THE
NANCY DREW
NOTEBOOKS®

#41

Flower Power

CAROLYN KEENE
ILLUSTRATED BY JAN NAIMO JONES

Published by Aladdin Paperbacks
New York   London   Toronto   Sydney   Singapore

This book is a work of fiction. Any references to historical events, real people, or real locales are used fictitiously. Other names, characters, places, and incidents are the product of the author's imagination, and any resemblance to actual events or locales or persons, living or dead, is entirely coincidental.

First Aladdin Paperbacks edition January 2002
First Minstrel Books edition April 2001

ALADDIN PAPERBACKS
An imprint of Simon & Schuster
Children's Publishing Division
1230 Avenue of the Americas
New York, NY 10020

The text of this book was set in Excelsior.

Printed in the U.S.A.
10 9 8 7 6 5 4 3 2

ISBN 0-7434-0664-8

1

The Flower Show

"Aren't these the most beautiful flowers you've ever seen?"

Eight-year-old Bess Marvin was sitting in the backseat of the Fayne family's car. She held up a flowerpot containing a bunch of frilly pink daisies.

Nancy Drew, who was sitting next to her, nodded. "Definitely! I think we're going to win first prize."

"I *know* we're going to win first prize," George Fayne piped up from the front seat. George's real name was Georgia. She and Bess were cousins, and Nancy's two best friends.

Mrs. Fayne, who was driving the car, smiled at her daughter. "Now, don't you girls get your hopes up too high. You're facing a lot of competition, you know."

"No problem," George said. "Our Pink Princess daisies rule!"

"Yeah!" Bess agreed.

Nancy giggled. George and Bess were right. Their Pink Princess daisies really *were* the best.

Mrs. Fayne was the vice president of the River Heights Garden Club. The club was sponsoring a flower show at the Civic Center. The show was opening in just three days.

Lots of prizes were going to be given at the flower show. There were two special children's prizes for flowers grown from seed: Most Beautiful Flower and Most Original Flower.

Three months earlier—way back in winter—Mrs. Fayne had tried to convince George to grow a flower for the show. At first George hadn't been too excited about the idea. She was more into sports than flowers and gardening.

Then one day Nancy, Bess, and their friend Julia Santos had been at George's house. The four of them happened to leaf through one of Mrs. Fayne's seed catalogs. They saw an ad for a rare type of daisy called the Pink Princess daisy. It was being sold with a limited-time offer. That meant that they could buy the seeds only for a short amount of time.

Right then and there, they decided to pool their money, order the seeds, and enter the contest together.

Now it was April, and the daisies were in full bloom. Nancy, George, Bess, and Julia had been passing the pot around for the last three months to water and fertilize it. Bess had had it for the past week, during most of the girls' spring vacation from school. Now it was Julia's turn.

"Here we are at the Civic Center!" Mrs. Fayne announced, turning the car into the parking lot.

Mrs. Fayne was going to help the other garden club members set up for the flower show. George and her friends would get a sneak peek at the exhibit.

Julia's mom was driving Julia there separately. The four girls planned to meet in the lobby.

The Civic Center was a big, important-looking building in downtown River Heights. An enormous green, pink, and white banner was draped across the front of it. It said:

THIS FRIDAY, SATURDAY, AND SUNDAY
THE FLOWER SHOW
SPONSORED BY THE RIVER HEIGHTS
GARDEN CLUB

Nancy felt a shiver of excitement as she got out of the car. She had never entered a flower contest before. Entering this one would be extra-fun because she was doing it with her friends.

As Mrs. Fayne and the girls walked into the Civic Center, Bess hugged the Pink Princess daisies to her chest. George turned to Bess and said, "Why did you bring them here, anyway? The flower show doesn't open for three more days."

"I don't like to let them out of my

sight," Bess said. "What if something happens to them?"

George rolled her eyes. "Oh, brother."

"Besides, I told Julia I'd bring them with me. That way she can take them home with her," Bess went on. "It's her turn to take care of them, until Friday."

Just then Nancy spotted Julia standing in the corner of the lobby. Julia waved and rushed up to Nancy and her friends. "Hi!" she said, smiling.

"Hi," Nancy said, smiling back.

Julia reached out to take the daisies from Bess. "Here, I'll take them now."

But Bess clung to the pot. "Uh, that's okay," she said. "I can carry them until we're all ready to go home."

Julia looked a little surprised. "Okay, whatever," she said, shrugging.

"This way, girls," Mrs. Fayne called out. She was heading through a set of double doors at the far end of the lobby. Nancy and her friends followed her.

On the other side of the double doors was the exhibit hall, where the flower show would be taking place. The hall was

a beehive of activity. Dozens of people were setting up exhibits.

Nancy took a deep breath. It smelled like a florist shop—times ten!

Right near the double doors was an especially cool display. Nancy noticed it right away. It was a garden with the words *River Heights* spelled out with pink and yellow roses.

Actually, it just said *River Height*. A young guy was still shaping the *S* with some pink roses.

"Excuse me, girls," Mrs. Fayne said. "I see Mrs. Van Hall over there. She's the president of the garden club, and I need to speak to her. Why don't you take a look around?"

"Okay, Mom," George said, nodding eagerly.

The four girls started wandering around the exhibit hall. They saw all kinds of pretty displays. There were trees that had been trimmed to look like elephants, giraffes, and other animals. There were big, fancy gardens with stone statues and trickling fountains.

6

"I've never seen a garden that was *indoors*," Bess remarked.

"Me, neither," Nancy said.

Nancy glanced around. She had never seen so many flowers in one place! She didn't know the names of all of them, but she recognized some from her own yard. There were purple irises and yellow daffodils and pink peonies. There were tulips of all colors.

There were also daisies. But nowhere in sight was there a Pink Princess daisy.

"Look!" Julia said, pointing. "That sign! It says, Children's Exhibits."

"Hey, that's our section!" Nancy said excitedly. "Let's check it out!"

Nancy and her friends headed across the exhibit hall. There were a couple of long tables under the Children's Exhibits sign. On one table was a sign that said Category: Most Beautiful Flower. On the other table was a sign that said Category: Most Original Flower.

"That's us," Bess said, skipping over to the first table. "Most Beautiful Flower.

Our Pink Princess daisy is going to win first prize!"

A girl was standing next to the Most Beautiful Flower table. She had long red hair and a freckled face, and she was wearing a yellow dress with polka dots all over it.

The girl glared at the pot of Pink Princess daisies in Bess's hands. "*My* flower is going to win first prize," she said in a mean voice. "Not yours!"

2

An Orson Encounter

Bess pouted at the redheaded girl. "What do you mean, *your* flower is going to win first prize? No way!"

"Yes, way," the girl retorted, putting her hands on her hips. "*My* flower for the Most Beautiful Flower contest is going to make *your* flower look like a bunch of weeds!"

"Viola! That's not a very nice thing to say!" George spoke up.

Nancy, Julia, and Bess all stared at George. "You *know* her?" Bess demanded.

George sighed. "This is Viola Van Hall. Her mom's the president of the garden

club. Viola, these are my friends Nancy Drew and Julia Santos, and my cousin Bess Marvin."

"You don't go to Carl Sandburg Elementary, do you?" Nancy asked Viola, trying to be friendly.

Viola sniffed. "Carl Sandburg? I don't think so. I go to Belvedere Academy. It's a private school."

Just then Mrs. Fayne walked up. With her was a tall woman with red hair that was pulled back in a ponytail. She was wearing a blue silk dress with a diamond pin shaped like a rose.

"Everyone, this is Mrs. Van Hall, the president of the garden club," Mrs. Fayne said. "Priscilla, this is my daughter, George; my niece, Bess; and their friends Nancy and Julia."

"Hello, girls," Mrs. Van Hall said.

Mrs. Fayne turned to George and Viola. "Isn't this a nice surprise! You girls seem to be really hitting it off."

"What?" George said, her brown eyes wide.

Mrs. Fayne smiled. "Well, we saw you

11

from across the room, and you were just gabbing and gabbing! Priscilla and I had given up hope that the two of you would ever be friends."

"I mean, you two girls have so much in common, with your interest in flowers and gardening and all," Mrs. Van Hall pointed out. "In fact, I have a wonderful idea! Why don't you come to our house tomorrow afternoon for tea—all of you. Viola and I can give you a tour of the garden."

Nancy, Bess, George, and Julia quickly exchanged glances. Nancy knew what her friends were thinking: How could they get out of this? Tea with mean, snobby Viola didn't sound like much fun at all!

"Oh, you mustn't say no," Mrs. Van Hall said cheerfully, as if reading their minds. "Besides our cook makes the most marvelous pastries. Raspberry tarts, lemon cakes . . ."

"I'm free!" Bess said immediately. Nancy knew that Bess could never say no to yummy food.

"I'm free, too," Nancy said politely. "Thank you for inviting us." George, her mother, and Julia agreed to go, too.

Maybe it won't be so bad, Nancy thought. Maybe Viola isn't as mean and snobby as she seems.

One of the other garden club members came over to ask Mrs. Van Hall about something. While the grown-ups talked, Viola leaned over to George and said in a low voice, "Just because my mom invited you to tea doesn't mean we're going to be friends." With that, she turned on her heels and walked away.

"What is her story?" Bess asked George as soon as Viola was out of earshot. "Why does she act like that?"

George shrugged. "I don't know. Our moms are always trying to make us play together. But I don't want to play with her. I don't like her!"

"I don't blame you," Julia said.

Just then Nancy noticed a familiar figure nearby: a boy with short black hair and brown eyes. He was slowly making his way down the aisle and checking out

all the booths. He was scribbling in a notebook and looking very intense.

The boy was Orson Wong. Orson was in the girls' third-grade class.

"Hey, Orson!" Nancy called out, waving.

Orson's head shot up. "You're breaking my concentration!" he complained.

"What are you concentrating on?" Bess asked him.

"I can't talk about it," Orson replied in a low voice. "It's a very special, top secret project."

Then Orson's eyes fell on the pot of Pink Princess daisies. "What are those?" he asked curiously.

"These are our Pink Princess daisies." Bess said proudly. "It's a really rare kind of daisy, and we grew them from these really hard-to-get seeds."

"We're going to win first prize for Most Beautiful Flower," Julia added.

"Hmm. A rare kind of daisy. Hard-to-get seeds." Orson began scribbling like mad in his notebook. "Would it be possible for me to take a sample?" He reached a hand toward the pot Bess was holding,

as if he were going to pluck one of the daisy buds off its stem.

Bess yanked the pot away from him. "Hey! Don't you dare!" she cried out.

Orson drew his hand back. "Um, sorry," he mumbled. He scribbled something else in his notebook. "A daisy with frilly pink petals," he said to himself as he wrote. "Excellent specimen."

"What are you talking about, Orson?" Julia asked him.

Orson looked up and smiled. "Everything will be revealed by the end of the week," he said mysteriously. "Good day, ladies! My mom's waiting for me at the begonia exhibit." He closed his notebook and continued down the aisle.

"What was that all about?" Bess asked Nancy.

"I don't know," Nancy said, staring after Orson. "But he's up to something."

The next morning at breakfast, Nancy told her father about her visit to the Civic Center.

"You wouldn't believe it, Daddy," she

said, her blue eyes shining. "The whole place was filled with pretty flowers!"

Carson Drew took a sip of coffee and smiled. "I believe it, Pudding Pie. And I bet your flower was the prettiest one in the whole place." Pudding Pie was Mr. Drew's special nickname for Nancy.

Nancy sighed. "I hope so. We really, really want to win first prize."

Hannah Gruen came over to the table just then, carrying a plate of steaming-hot blueberry pancakes. She had been the Drews' housekeeper for the last five years, since Nancy's mother died.

"Who wants more pancakes?" Hannah asked.

Nancy raised her hand. "I do, I do!"

Carson raised his hand, too. "That makes two of us, Hannah," he said. He added, "Nancy was just telling me about the flower show."

"Oh, I know all about it," Hannah said, winking. "I've been watching those Pink Princess daisies grow since January." She set the plate down on the table. "Didn't you tell me there were two categories for

17

the children's prizes, Nancy? The one you're in, and another one?"

Nancy speared a bunch of pancakes onto her plate and nodded. "Most Beautiful Flower and Most Original Flower. I guess Most Original means 'weirdest' or something."

Carson laughed. "Or something."

"But all we care about is the Most Beautiful Flower category, because that's the one we're going to win!" Nancy said excitedly.

Carson winked at Hannah. "That's enthusiasm for you."

The phone began ringing. Hannah answered it and then handed the phone to Nancy. "It's for you."

Nancy took the phone from Hannah. "Hello?"

"Um, hello . . . Nancy?"

Nancy recognized Julia's voice right away. Julia sounded upset about something.

"Julia? What's wrong?" Nancy asked her.

"Oh, Nancy. It's terrible! It's the worst

thing in the whole wide world!" Julia cried out.

"What?" Nancy asked her, alarmed.

"The Pink Princess daisies!" Julia exclaimed. "They're gone!"

3

An Emergency Meeting

Julia! What do you mean, the Pink Princess daisies are gone?" Nancy demanded.

Out of the corner of her eye, Nancy saw that her father and Hannah had stopped eating their blueberry pancakes and were staring at her.

"What's going on, Nancy?" Hannah whispered to her.

Nancy shrugged. "I'm not sure," she whispered back.

"Yesterday? When we got back from the Civic Center?" Julia went on, sounding really upset. "I put the pot of daisies on

20

our back porch. You know, so they could get some sun and stuff?"

"Then what happened?" Nancy prompted her.

"I didn't bring them inside last night, because it was so warm," Julia replied. "My mom always said that was good for potted plants to spend nights outside as long as it wasn't cold or anything. Anyway." She took a deep breath. "I went outside this morning to check on them. And they were totally gone!"

"Maybe your mom or your dad moved them," Nancy suggested.

"No, I asked them. They didn't have a clue," Julia replied. She sniffled, as if she was about to start crying. "I'm really, really sorry, Nancy! I lost our daisies!"

Nancy thought for a moment. "We'll find them," she said finally. "I'm not sure how, but we'll find them. I'm going to call Bess and George right now. It's time for an emergency meeting!"

"I can't believe you lost our Pink Princess daisies!" Bess moaned to Julia.

Bess, Julia, Nancy, and George were sitting on the Santoses' deck. The deck overlooked the backyard, which was big and L-shaped. The yard had a lawn lined with bushes and flower beds.

The girls were gathered around a picnic table on the deck. The sun was warm on their faces, and they had a pitcher of lemonade and a plate of banana muffins to share. Still, they were all grumpy because of the missing daisies.

"I'm sorry, I'm sorry, I'm sorry," Julia said, for what seemed like the hundredth time.

"Nancy's the best detective at Carl Sandburg Elementary," George said calmly. "She'll find the daisies."

"Only if you guys help," Nancy said.

She reached into her pocket and got out her special blue notebook. Her father had given it to her for writing down clues when she was on a case.

Nancy really liked solving mysteries. And this was a really, really important mystery. Their Pink Princess daisies were missing, and the flower show was only

two days away! They *had* to find the daisies, since there was no time to grow more of them from seeds.

Nancy got out her favorite purple pen, turned to a fresh page in the blue notebook, and wrote: The Case of the Missing Daisies.

She glanced up at her friends. "Do we have any suspects?" she said.

"Suspects!" Bess exclaimed. "So you think someone stole the daisies?"

Nancy nodded. "Definitely. I mean, they didn't just walk off by themselves."

Bess crossed her arms over her chest. "Maybe Julia forgot them somewhere," she said huffily.

"No! I swear! I left them right here on the deck—over there, by the railing." Julia pointed to a spot on the deck floor, near a pot of yellow pansies. "The daisies were there yesterday afternoon," Julia went on. "And they were totally gone when I got up this morning."

"I just thought of someone who might be a suspect," George spoke up. "Orson Wong! He was acting really weird yesterday."

"Orson is *always* acting weird," Bess pointed out.

George shrugged. "Whatever. But he tried to take one of the daisies from you, remember? And he was talking about specimens."

Nancy nodded. "Specimens. Like he wanted the daisies for a scientific experiment or something." She added, "Orson's always doing scientific experiments."

Bess gasped. "My beautiful daisies! You mean, he could be blowing them up or pouring chemicals on them or something?"

"I don't know," Nancy replied. After all, they couldn't be sure that Orson was the thief—not until they had some proof.

Nancy picked up her purple pen and wrote down Orson's name under Suspects.

Then something occurred to Nancy. "What about that girl Viola?" she said. "She was so sure her flowers were going to win the Most Beautiful Flower prize."

Julia took a sip of lemonade. "Yeah. Maybe she was going to make extra-sure about that—by stealing our daisies!"

Nancy wrote Viola's name down under Orson's. "We're going over to Viola's house later for tea, right? We can look for the daisies while we're there," she suggested.

"Good idea," George said.

"Helllooo! Yoo-hoo!"

Nancy glanced up. A woman with long, curly blond hair and tiny gold wire-rimmed glasses was walking across the Santoses' yard toward them.

The woman was dressed in a loose cotton dress that had a really crazy flower and butterfly pattern on it. Nancy got dizzy just staring at it.

"Hi, Mrs. Bridges," Julia called out. "She's our next-door neighbor," she whispered to Nancy and her friends.

"Greetings, ladies! What a lovely day!" Mrs. Bridges walked up to the picnic table. Nancy saw that she was wearing green cotton gloves with lots of dirt on them.

Mrs. Bridges smiled at Nancy, Bess, and George. "I don't believe I've had the pleasure. I'm Belle Bridges."

"Hi, Mrs. Bridges," Nancy said. She

introduced herself, and George and Bess did the same.

"Julia, dear. I left my little antique watering can here when I came by to say hello yesterday," Mrs. Bridges said, glancing around. "Oh, there it is." She reached under the picnic table and picked up a silver watering can.

"Are you a gardener, too?" Nancy asked Mrs. Bridges.

Mrs. Bridges sighed dramatically. "Oh, yes. A *passionate* gardener. Also a writer and gourmet chef. I always say, one should never limit oneself to just one occupation."

"Gourmet chef," Bess repeated. "You mean, as in, you cook really yummy food?"

Mrs. Bridges laughed. "Exactly."

The four girls chatted with Mrs. Bridges for a few more minutes. Then Mrs. Bridges said goodbye and headed back to her house, watering can in hand.

Nancy noticed that Julia was staring after her with a funny expression. "What is it, Julia?" Nancy asked her curiously.

Julia frowned. "I'm not sure. But I just remembered something. When Mrs. Bridges came by yesterday, she saw the Pink Princess daisies on the deck. She asked me lots of questions about them."

"Questions? Like what?" George asked her.

"She told me that she was writing an article about edible flowers for some food magazine," Julia explained. "Edible, as in, you can eat them. I guess you can eat some flowers, in salads and stuff."

"Flowers in salad? Yuck!" Bess said, making a face.

"Anyway, Mrs. Bridges was asking me if the Pink Princess daisies were edible, and how could she get some," Julia went on. "She said . . . she said they would look really beautiful in a salad."

"A salad!" Nancy repeated. She had a sudden, bad feeling. "Oh, no! What if Mrs. Bridges stole our Pink Princess daisies and has eaten them already?"

4

Tea with Viola

Bess gasped. "You mean, Mrs. Bridges stole our Pink Princess daisies and cut them all up into tiny eensy-weensy little pieces and made a salad out of them?" she cried out.

"That is so awful!" George agreed.

"I think I'm going to cry," Julia said. Her lip was quivering.

Nancy waved her pen in the air. "Wait, guys. We can't be sure if Mrs. Bridges stole the daisies for a salad. We have to get some proof first."

Julia sniffed. "H-how do we do that?"

Nancy chewed the end of her pen

thoughtfully. "Hmm. I know! Julia, can you get us invited to Mrs. Bridges's house?"

"I guess so," Julia said. She sounded a little doubtful, though. "What will I tell her?"

"I have an idea!" George said eagerly. "Tell her that we want to do a group report on edible flowers for school."

"Yeah!" Bess piped up. "Tell her we want to interview her or something."

"Okay," Julia said, nodding. "I can do that."

"That's a great idea, George," Nancy said excitedly. "And while we're in her house, we can look around for our daisies and ask her questions."

"Sounds good." Bess reached for the plate of banana muffins. "All this talk about edible stuff is making me hungry."

". . . And these over here are called astilbe," Mrs. Van Hall explained. "Notice their fine, feathery blossoms. And as you can see, we have three varieties: white, pink, and red . . ."

It was Wednesday afternoon. Mrs. Van Hall was leading Mrs. Fayne, George, Nancy, Bess, and Julia through the Van Halls' garden.

Viola was there, too. But she was hanging back, looking kind of grumpy.

Everyone was dressed up for tea. Mrs. Van Hall and Mrs. Fayne were wearing nice skirts and blouses. All the girls were wearing dresses.

The Van Halls lived in an enormous gray stone mansion. It had so many windows that Nancy couldn't even count them. She thought that the house looked kind of like a castle.

The garden was enormous, too, with flowers everywhere. Plus, there were statues, fountains, and long, winding paths. There was even an antique sundial.

As they walked, George leaned over to Nancy and whispered, "This is, like, a hundred times bigger than your garden and my garden and Bess's garden and Julia's garden put together."

"Definitely," Nancy said.

After the garden tour, Mrs. Van Hall led

everyone back to the terrace. There were seven places set for tea, with pretty china plates and cups.

In the middle of the table was a big silver teapot, pitchers of jam and cream, and trays of delicious things to eat: scones, cakes, tarts, and tiny ham and cucumber sandwiches. There was also a big vase of white and yellow daisies.

But not pink, Nancy noticed.

"Well, isn't this lovely?" Mrs. Fayne said, clapping her hands together.

"Oh, it's nothing," Mrs. Van Hall said modestly. "Viola and George, why don't you sit together right over here?" She pointed to two chairs at the end of the table.

George threw a quick glance at Nancy, as if to say, "Help!" Nancy shrugged and smiled sympathetically.

Nancy sat down between Julia and Bess. While everyone was getting comfortable, Julia whispered to Nancy, "It's all set. I talked to Mrs. Bridges about our, um, report on edible flowers. She invited us all to lunch tomorrow."

"That's great," Nancy whispered back.

Mrs. Van Hall poured tea out of the silver teapot for everyone. Nancy took a sip. It tasted like peppermint, and it was delicious.

When the grown-ups started talking about gardening, Nancy switched her attention to Viola.

Viola was putting some cream and jam on a scone. Nancy watched her, then did the same. It was really yummy. She also tried a thin little ham and cucumber sandwich. It was really yummy, too.

Nancy was so busy eating that she almost forgot about the plan.

She jumped up from her chair. "Um, may I be excused? I need to find the, um, rest room."

Mrs. Van Hall smiled at her. "Of course, Nancy. Go in through the double doors. The guest bathroom is down the hall and to the left."

"Thank you, Mrs. Van Hall," Nancy said. She started toward the double doors, then paused and turned around for a second. The grown-ups had gone back to their

conversation. Viola was busily attacking a raspberry tart with her silver fork.

Bess, George, and Julia were all watching Nancy. Bess gave Nancy a thumbs-up sign. George and Julia did, too.

Nancy turned and went inside the house. It was as fancy on the inside as it was on the outside. The floors were made of dark, polished wood, and there was antique furniture everywhere. On the walls were lots of paintings, like in a museum.

Nancy made her way down the hall. She passed the guest bathroom on the left. She continued down the hall until she found the stairs going to the second floor.

She glanced around. As far as she could tell, she was all alone. She went up the stairs very quietly. That was hard to do because they were made of marble. The soles of her black patent-leather shoes slapped noisily against the steps.

Once she got to the second floor, Nancy glanced around again. How was she ever going to find Viola's room? she wondered.

There were many doors on each side of the long hallway.

"I guess I should just start peeking in all the doors," Nancy said to herself.

Fortunately, most of the doors were open. Nancy peeked in on one fancy room after another.

Finally, she reached a bedroom that looked like it could be Viola's. It had a white wicker bed with lots of dolls neatly propped up against the pillows. There were framed posters of unicorns on the walls, which were covered with a violet-pattern wallpaper.

Nancy glanced around quickly, then went into the bedroom and half-closed the door behind her. She started searching for the Pink Princess daisies.

There were some potted flowers on the windowsill, but they weren't daisies. Nancy looked in the closet and under the bed and under the desk. But still, she didn't see the Pink Princess daisies.

Then she noticed something on top of the desk. It was a seed catalog. It was the same one Mrs. Fayne had had—the one

from which Nancy and her friends had ordered their Pink Princess daisy seeds.

Nancy opened the catalog. The page about the Pink Princess daisies had a purple bookmark in it!

Just then a voice called out from behind her, "What are you doing in my room?"

5

A Pink Princess Salad?

Nancy whirled around at the sound of the familiar voice. Viola was standing in the doorway. Her hands were on her hips, and she looked really, really mad.

"I said, what are you doing in my room, Nancy Drew?" Viola repeated.

Uh-oh, Nancy thought. Busted!

She wondered what had happened to the plan. Bess, George, and Julia were supposed to keep Viola busy on the terrace. That way Nancy could search for the daisies in peace.

There was a noise in the hallway behind

Viola. Bess's, George's, and Julia's heads suddenly appeared.

"Oh, *there* you are, Nancy!" Bess said in a too-bright voice.

"Viola was worried that you'd gotten lost or something, so we came looking for you," George added.

"You didn't get lost, Nancy, you came up here to snoop around my bedroom!" Viola accused.

"Th-that's not true," Nancy said, thinking quickly. "I couldn't find the bathroom your mom was talking about, so I came upstairs."

Just then Nancy noticed a fuzzy cat toy on the floor. It gave her an idea.

"So, um, I came upstairs," Nancy repeated. "Then, um, as I was passing this door, I thought I heard a cat meowing inside. I wanted to let it out."

Nancy waited, holding her breath, hoping that Viola would believe her crazy made-up story.

"Maximilian was stuck in here?" Viola said, glancing around. "Again? Where is he?"

Good, she really does have a cat, Nancy thought, relieved. Out loud, she said, "I think he went down the hall."

Viola peered out into the hallway. "Maximilian!" she called out. "Come here, kitty kitty!"

"Your room is really pretty," Nancy said, trying to change the subject.

Viola turned around and stared at her. "What? Oh, thanks."

"You have a lot of cool stuff," Nancy went on. "Oh, and I noticed you have a seed catalog on your desk. George's mom has the same one. We ordered the seeds for our Pink Princess daisies from it."

Nancy watched Viola, to see how she would act at the mention of the daisies. Nancy also wondered if Viola would explain why she had a bookmark at the Pink Princess daisy page.

But Viola didn't explain anything. Instead, she marched across the room, picked up the catalog, and stuffed it into a desk drawer. "I don't appreciate people going through my stuff," she said, her

green eyes blazing. "Okay, everybody out of my room!"

On their way downstairs, Nancy leaned over to Bess and whispered, "What happened? You guys were supposed to keep Viola busy."

"She had to go to the bathroom," Bess whispered back. "We didn't know what to do, so we all said we had to go to the bathroom, too. Then, when she didn't see you in the guest bathroom downstairs, she got suspicious and went to look for you."

"I'm just glad she believed my cat story," Nancy whispered.

"Do you think she has our daisies?" Bess whispered.

"I'm not sure," Nancy whispered back. "She *did* have the seed catalog—and she had a bookmark at the Pink Princess daisy page. I think that makes her our number one suspect!"

"You must be very, very careful when you're dealing with edible flowers," Belle Bridges told Nancy and her friends.

It was Thursday afternoon. Nancy, George, Julia, and Bess were sitting at Mrs. Bridges's dining room table, getting ready to have a lunch of edible flowers.

Today Mrs. Bridges was dressed in jeans and a big, baggy white T-shirt that said Flower Power on it.

Nancy could see that Mrs. Bridges was a serious plant lover. All the windows in her house had huge, droopy plants hanging in them. There were three huge bookshelves full of gardening books. On the walls were paintings of flowers—painted by Mrs. Bridges herself—and pots of flowers filled every windowsill and shelf and tabletop.

Nancy glanced around. There was no sign of the Pink Princess daisies anywhere.

"Why do you have to be careful with edible flowers?" Bess asked Mrs. Bridges. She had a notebook and pen in hand, and was taking notes for the pretend report.

"Because in addition to the edible flowers, there are a number of *inedible* flow-

ers," Mrs. Bridges explained. "Some of them are poisonous, even deadly!"

Julia's eyes grew wide. "You mean they can kill you?" she asked.

"Yes, indeed," Mrs. Bridges told the girls. "Take lily of the valley, for example. Those pretty little white bell-like blossoms that smell so lovely. If you happened to eat them by accident, you would have terrible stomach pains and hot flashes and maybe even die."

Nancy gulped. There were lilies of the valley in her yard at home. She had no idea they were deadly!

"There are all sorts of other flowers that can kill you," Mrs. Bridges went on. "There's foxglove and monkshood and oleander . . ."

Mrs. Bridges's words were starting to make Nancy shivery and goose-bumpy. She didn't like talking about poisonous flowers.

". . . and rhododendron. Shall I go on?" Mrs. Bridges asked.

"No!" the girls cried out together.

Mrs. Bridges smiled. "It's not a very

pleasant subject, is it? Still, it's important that you girls include this information in your report for school. In any case, it's time for me to serve lunch. It'll just take me a minute to get it ready."

Mrs. Bridges disappeared into the kitchen. Nancy leaned over and whispered to her friends, "I don't see the Pink Princess daisies anywhere."

"I saw a couple of empty flowerpots outside the front door when we came in," George whispered back. "I checked them to see if any of them was ours, like maybe she took the daisies out of it or something. But none of them had our initials on it."

Nancy and her friends had painted their initials in pink on the bottom of their pot: ND, BM, GF, and JS.

"Forget about the daisies for a minute!" Bess whispered frantically. "You don't think Mrs. Bridges is going to serve us poisonous flowers for lunch, do you?"

"Bess, that's crazy!" George whispered.

"Girls! Lunch is served!"

Nancy's head snapped up. Mrs. Bridges

44

was standing in the doorway, holding a big wooden bowl.

"I've made us a very special salad today," Mrs. Bridges said with a smile. "A very special salad with some very special edible flowers. *Pink* edible flowers!"

Bess gasped. Nancy, George, and Julia exchanged a glance.

Nancy knew they were all thinking the exact same thing.

Was Mrs. Bridges going to serve them their Pink Princess daisies for lunch?

6

The Flower Experiment

Nancy was tingling with worry as Mrs. Bridges walked over to the dining room table, bowl in hand.

Would the bowl contain chopped-up pieces of their precious daisies? Nancy wondered.

Mrs. Bridges set down the bowl in the middle of the table. Nancy and her friends all sat up in their chairs and leaned forward, trying to make out what was inside the bowl.

Nancy closed her eyes for a second. She was afraid of what she would see.

She took a deep breath and opened her

eyes. Inside the bowl was lettuce . . . and spinach . . . and tomatoes . . . and cucumber slices . . .

. . . and some little pink flowers.

But the little pink flowers didn't look anything like their daisies, Nancy realized. The petals were smaller and a different shade of pink altogether.

Nancy sighed with relief. So did George, Bess, and Julia.

"What are these flowers?" Julia asked Mrs. Bridges, as if to make one-hundred-percent sure.

"Pink violets!" Mrs. Bridges said proudly. "They're rather unusual, aren't they? Usually violets are purple, but these are a special pink variety that I grow in my backyard."

"Are they edible?" Bess asked her cautiously.

Mrs. Bridges laughed. "Of course! The violet is one of the most common edible flowers."

Mrs. Bridges served the salad to the girls on pretty yellow salad plates. Nancy picked up her fork and speared one of the

pink violets. She put it in her mouth and tasted it.

It's different, Nancy thought, munching. Kind of yummy, but kind of weird, too.

"Mmm, this is good!" Bess said, popping a couple of pink violets into her mouth. "I'll have to tell my mom and dad to start putting edible flowers in *our* salads."

Fifteen minutes later everyone had cleaned their plates. Mrs. Bridges went back into the kitchen and returned with bowls of reddish pink ice cream.

"Dessert!" she announced cheerfully.

Bess picked up her spoon. "Mmm, strawberry ice cream!" she said excitedly.

"Actually, it's red geranium sorbet," Mrs. Bridges corrected her. "The red geranium is another edible flower. I made the sorbet myself, from scratch. I grow the geraniums in a window box."

"Red geranium sorbet," Bess repeated. "Hmm. Okay, well, it *looks* like ice cream, so it must be all right."

As the five of them dug into the sorbet, a young guy came into the dining room.

Nancy guessed that he was about eighteen or so. He had long, greasy blond hair and glasses, and he was dressed in baggy shorts and a T-shirt.

"Byron, hello!" Mrs. Bridges called out. "Girls, this is my son, Byron. Byron, this is Nancy, George, and Bess—and of course you know Julia."

"Hey," Byron mumbled.

"Byron works part-time doing odd jobs for Julia's parents," Mrs. Bridges told Nancy, George, and Bess. "You know, fixing things around the house, helping out with the yard, and so forth. The rest of the time, he's going to college. He's majoring in . . . what is it you're majoring in these days, dear?"

"I don't know, drama or astrophysics or whatever," Byron replied, stuffing his hands in his pockets. "Got anything to eat?"

"Could I interest you in a mixed green salad with pink violets and some red geranium sorbet?" Mrs. Bridges said brightly.

Byron made a face. "Uh, no, thanks,

Mom. I think I'll go over to the Quik-E-Burger instead."

After Byron left, Mrs. Bridges frowned and said, "That boy has no taste at all. He's always eating those horribly unnatural pretend-food products."

Nancy liked Quik-E-Burgers, but she didn't think it would be polite to say so. Instead, she said, "Mrs. Bridges? Julia said you were interested in our Pink Princess daisies."

Mrs. Bridges looked startled. "Oh, yes, those flowers you had out the other day, Julia." She paused. "I thought they were edible, so I looked them up in one of my books. It turns out they're not edible."

"They're not edible?" Bess said happily. Nancy knew what her friend was thinking: Maybe this meant Mrs. Bridges didn't steal them to put in a salad, after all.

"No, they're not edible," Mrs. Bridges replied. "More red geranium sorbet, anyone?"

As Nancy ate her second helping of sorbet, she thought: Maybe this meant they

could cross Mrs. Bridges off their suspect list.

That meant they had only two suspects left: Viola Van Hall and Orson Wong.

"Orson's in his room. You can go on up, girls," Mr. Wong said.

Nancy, George, Bess, and Julia went up the stairs to Orson's room. His twin brothers, Lonny and Lenny, who were six, were running around the living room, having a pretend-battle with umbrellas.

"Lonny! Lenny! Umbrellas aren't toys!" Nancy heard Mr. Wong scolding them.

When they got to Orson's room, they found the door closed. Nancy knocked.

"Enter!" came Orson's voice.

Nancy opened the door and went inside. The other girls followed.

The shades were drawn, and the room was almost totally dark.

Nancy glanced around, trying to get her bearings. She had been in Orson's room before. He had all kinds of interesting things in it. There was a big blue globe on his dresser and a bug mobile hanging

from the ceiling. Orson's pet iguana was very still in his cage, looking at everything with big, bulging eyes.

Orson was sitting at his desk, which was usually covered with rocks and minerals and plastic dinosaurs. Today, though, it was covered with pots of really weird-looking flowers. A lamp was shining an eerie bluish white light on the flowers.

Orson's desk looks like the laboratory of a mad scientist, Nancy thought.

"Orson?" Nancy said. She blinked, trying to adjust her eyes to the strange bluish white light in the room.

Orson turned around in his chair. "Welcome!" he called out. "Don't turn on the light—my subjects are very sensitive!"

"What are you doing?" Bess demanded. "Why is it dark, and what's up with that weird blue light, and what are those mutant flowers on your desk?"

"Interesting you should ask," Orson said, rubbing his hands together. "I have been conducting a series of cross-pollination and hybridization experiments."

"Cross-what? And hybri-what?" Julia asked him.

"Basically, I'm creating new breeds of flowers by mixing up the old breeds," Orson explained.

Nancy stared at the flowers on his desk. They were really, really strange-looking. One of them was an oversize yellow flower with a fuzzy purple middle and jagged leaves. Another one had two flowers—a pink flower and a totally different-looking red flower—coming out of one stem.

George was staring at the flowers on Orson's desk, too. "Orson, that is insane!" she exclaimed.

"Not at all," Orson said calmly. "Cross-pollination and hybridization are common techniques. Scientists and gardeners use them to create new kinds of flowers."

Nancy moved closer to Orson's desk to get a better look at the flowers. All of a sudden, she noticed something. Something bad.

One of the flowers way in the back looked like the Pink Princess daisy.

Except that this one had an ugly, spiky red thing sticking out of the middle of it.

Nancy felt all queasy in her stomach.

Did Orson steal our Pink Princess daisies and do a scientific experiment on them? she wondered.

7

A Surprise Suspect

Nancy moved closer to Orson's desk. For a second she squeezed her eyes shut. She couldn't bear to see what Orson had done to their Pink Princess daisies.

If Orson turned our daisies into some sort of horrible, yucky mutant flowers, I'll never forgive him! Nancy thought.

She opened her eyes. She bent down and took a long, hard look at the weird pink flower.

But it wasn't pink at all. It just looked that way under the bluish white light.

"Nancy? What is it?" Bess asked her.

Nancy turned around. "Nothing. I just

thought I saw something . . . familiar." She glanced at Orson. "Listen, Orson. Remember those Pink Princess daisies we showed you at the Civic Center the other day?"

Orson reached for a notebook and flipped to the middle of it. "Yes, of course, here it is. 'A rare kind of daisy. Hard-to-get seeds. Frilly pink petals. Excellent specimen.'"

"You haven't seen any of them around, have you?" George asked him pointedly.

Orson shrugged. "Of course not. They're rare, aren't they? *Rare* means you don't see them around." His eyes gleamed. "However, I would love to borrow your Pink Princess daisies after the flower show is over. They would make excellent specimens for a new cross-pollination experiment I'm designing."

"Ewww!" Bess cried out. "You are *not* going to cross-polli-whatever our Pink Princess daisies!"

"Let's go," Nancy whispered to her friends. "I don't think Orson knows anything about the daisies."

"Yeah, let's get out of here," Julia whispered back.

"Just think about my offer!" Orson called out as the girls turned to go. "You would be making a valuable contribution to science!"

Bess stuck a spoon into her Crazy Creamy Caramel Sundae. "Tomorrow is the opening day of the flower show. And we still haven't found our daisies!" she moaned.

Bess, Nancy, George, and Julia had decided to discuss the case at the Double Dip. The Double Dip was their favorite ice cream place in River Heights. Julia's mom had dropped them off, and Bess's mom was going to pick them up.

George took a bite of her Blueberry Burst Sundae. "I guess we should just give up," she said with a sad sigh. "We're not going to have an entry in the flower show, after all."

"We can't give up yet!" Nancy cried out. She pulled out her special blue notebook and turned to the page about the missing daisies.

"We can cross Mrs. Bridges off the suspect list," Nancy said, scanning the page. "Orson doesn't seem like a really good suspect anymore, either. We didn't see the daisies in his room. And he asked to borrow them after the flower show is over."

"Which means that he probably doesn't have them now," Julia piped up. She peered over Nancy's shoulder at the entry in the blue notebook. "We still have Viola Van Hall," she said.

Nancy nodded. "That's kind of a dead end for now, though. Viola doesn't want to talk to us."

"She is so mean," George complained.

Nancy took a bite of her Strawberry Surprise Sundae. Were they missing an important clue in this case? she wondered. Why couldn't they find the daisies?

Nancy glanced up at Julia. "Let's go back to the scene of the crime," she suggested. "Try to remember what happened when you put the daisies on your deck Tuesday afternoon. Try to remember everything . . . every little detail."

"I've seen detectives do stuff like that

on TV," Julia said, nodding. She closed her eyes. "Okay. I came home from the Civic Center with my mom. She went into the kitchen to start dinner. I took the daisies to the deck. I put them next to a bunch of other flowerpots—pansies and begonias and geraniums and stuff. And then Mrs. Bridges came by, and—"

"Wait!" Nancy interrupted her. "What do you mean, you put them next to a bunch of other flowerpots? They weren't there yesterday—except maybe one pot of yellow pansies, I think."

Julia opened her eyes and blinked. "You're right, Nancy," she said slowly. "Come to think of it, those flowerpots weren't there the next morning, either. Except for the yellow pansies."

Nancy took another spoonful of her sundae. "Then this might be a brand-new case," she announced. "Maybe the thief wasn't just after the Pink Princess daisies, but all the other flowers, too!"

Nancy glanced up at the sky. It would be dark in about an hour or so.

She hurried her steps. The Santoses' house was just around the corner.

After the Double Dip, Mrs. Marvin had driven her and the other girls home. At her house, Nancy had started helping Hannah with dinner.

Then she thought about what Julia had said: That not just the daisies, but a bunch of other flowers, had disappeared sometime between Tuesday afternoon and Wednesday morning.

So Nancy had decided to go by the Santoses' house before dinnertime to do one last sweep for clues.

She soon reached the Santoses' front door and knocked. Julia's mother answered.

"Well, hello, Nancy," Mrs. Santos said with a smile.

Nancy smiled, too. "Hi, Mrs. Santos. Is Julia here?"

"She's out back," Mrs. Santos replied.

Nancy thanked her, then went around the house. She didn't see any sign of Julia.

Maybe she's way in the back of the

yard, Nancy thought. The Santoses' yard was large and L-shaped. It was impossible to see the whole yard from the deck.

Nancy started wandering around the yard, calling Julia's name. There was no reply. A fat yellow cat darted out of a bush and through her legs, startling her.

"Yow!" Nancy cried out. The cat disappeared into another bush.

Then Nancy noticed something. Next to the bush where the cat was hiding was a little patch of flowers. They looked as though they had just been planted. The dirt was freshly turned, and a small shovel was lying nearby.

Nancy did a double take. The flower patch included begonias. And pansies. And geraniums.

And some Pink Princess daisies!

Nancy took a closer look. They were definitely Pink Princess daisies—the missing Pink Princess daisies!

8

The Most Beautiful Flower

ancy stared at the Pink Princess daisies, totally confused. Why had Julia said that the daisies had been stolen? And why did Julia plant them in her own backyard?

"Hey, Nancy! What are you doing here?"

Nancy turned around. Julia was running across the yard toward her.

"Hi, Julia," Nancy said. She pointed to the Pink Princess daisies. "Look what I just found."

Nancy waited, watching for Julia's reaction. But instead of acting guilty or

upset, Julia smiled and started jumping up and down.

"The Pink Princess daisies!" she cried out. "Nancy, you found them! You found them!"

Now Nancy was totally confused. "Y-you didn't know they were here?" she stammered.

Julia frowned at Nancy. "Know? How could I know? This is a total and complete surprise. I mean, what are they doing here, in our garden?"

"Do you think that maybe your mom or your dad planted them here by accident?" Nancy asked her.

Julia shook her head. "I asked them about the daisies right away, as soon as I realized they were missing. They didn't know anything about them."

Just then something caught Nancy's eye. There was a crumpled-up piece of paper lying near the daisies.

Nancy bent down to pick it up. She smoothed it open. It was a Quik-E-Burger wrapper.

Quik-E-Burgers, as in what Byron Bridges likes to eat! Nancy thought.

Nancy grabbed Julia's arm. "Come on. We have to talk to Byron Bridges right away," she said.

"Why?" Julia asked curiously.

"You'll see!" Nancy told her.

The two of them found Byron and Mrs. Bridges in their backyard. Byron was playing a handheld computer game while Mrs. Bridges picked some flowers for dinner.

"Hello, ladies!" Mrs. Bridges called out when she saw Nancy and Julia. She wiped her forehead with the back of her gardening glove. "Tonight's menu is grilled salmon and nasturtium-blossom salad. Can you stay?"

"No, thank you," Nancy said quickly. "We need to talk to Byron."

Mrs. Bridges stared curiously at Nancy, and then at her son. "Byron? What for?"

"Byron, you do yardwork for the Santos family, right?" Nancy asked him.

Byron didn't glance up from his com-

puter game. "Yeah, what about it?" he said, pushing some buttons very fast.

"Did you happen to plant some pink daisies in their garden yesterday?" Nancy persisted.

"Were they on the deck in some pot or something?" Byron asked her.

"Yes," Nancy replied.

Byron finally glanced up from his computer game. "Not yesterday. Tuesday. I went to the Quik-E-Burger for a bacon cheeseburger, just before dinnertime . . ."

Mrs. Bridges made a face.

". . . and then I went next door to do some yardwork," Byron continued. "I saw a bunch of flowers on the back deck. I figured Mr. and Mrs. Santos wanted them planted, so I planted them." He frowned at Nancy and Julia. "What's the big deal? Is there a problem?"

Julia grinned. "Not anymore! Nancy just solved The Case of the Missing Daisies!"

"When are they going to announce the winners?" Bess said anxiously.

It was Sunday afternoon—the third and final day of the flower show. Nancy, Bess, George, and Julia were hanging out in the Children's Exhibits section, pacing nervously. Three judges were making their final decision on the Most Beautiful Flower and Most Original Flower prizes.

Carson Drew, Mr. and Mrs. Marvin, and the other parents were there, too. So were Hannah and Mrs. Bridges. Orson and his parents were there, too, as was Viola and her mother.

Viola kept glancing over at Nancy and her friends, and then at the judges. Nancy thought that she seemed kind of nervous.

Nancy had checked out Viola's entry earlier. It was also a kind of daisy, called a Golden Sun daisy. It was pretty, but not nearly as pretty as the Pink Princess daisy. That's what Nancy thought, anyway.

Carson came over and squeezed Nancy's shoulder. "How are you doing, Pudding Pie? Holding up under the pressure?"

Nancy nodded. "Yes, Daddy. I really,

really think we're going to win. But even if we don't, I'll still be glad that we found the daisies safe and sound."

"You're my little detective," he said, ruffling her hair affectionately.

"We have the winners!" one of the judges announced.

The crowd fell silent. Bess reached for Nancy's hand. Nancy reached for George's hand. George reached for Julia's hand. The four girls stood like that for what seemed like a really long time, waiting for the judges' decisions.

"The Most Original Flower prize goes to Contestant Number Thirteen for the Moonwalking Daffolily!" the judge announced.

Orson began jumping up and down. "That's me! That's me!" He went rushing up to the table and picked up a pot marked Number 13. He held it up in the air, like a trophy.

Nancy stared at it. Orson's Moonwalking Daffolily was the flower she'd seen on his desk, under the blue-white lamp. It was the oversize yellow flower

with the weird fuzzy purple middle and jagged leaves.

"My cross-pollination experiment was a success!" Orson hooted. "I win! I win!"

Mrs. Bridges walked up to Orson. She peered at the Moonwalking Daffolily over the rim of her glasses. "It's very interesting," she said to Orson. "Is it edible? Could I interview you for a piece I'm doing on edible flowers?"

"Sure!" Orson said happily.

Nancy turned her attention back to the judge. When was he going to announce the prize for their category? she wondered impatiently.

The judge cleared his throat. "The prize for the Most Beautiful Flower category is . . . Contestant Number Eight, for the Pink Princess daisy!"

The Pink Princess daisy! Nancy thought. That's us!

"Yes!" Bess shouted, and began jumping up and down. Nancy, George, and Julia began jumping up and down, too.

Carson Drew and the other girls' parents came up and congratulated them.

After a moment Viola shuffled up to them, too.

"Congratulations. I guess," Viola said.

Nancy and her friends stopped jumping. "Um, thanks," Nancy said to Viola. "Your flower was really pretty, too," she added, trying to be nice.

"What? Oh, I don't really care about that," Viola said, shrugging. "Actually, I'm glad this contest is over. My mom made me enter it," she said.

"Really?" George said. "My mom sort of did that, too."

"I guess our moms are really into gardening," Viola said.

George nodded. "Yeah. I mean, I kind of like it, too. But I'm much more into soccer and stuff."

Viola's face lit up. "You play soccer? Wow, that's really cool."

Nancy turned to Viola. "Viola, why did you have that seed catalog on your desk on Wednesday?" she asked.

Viola smiled and shrugged. "I know I told you guys that your daisies were ugly. But actually, I thought they were really

pretty. I wanted to order the seeds to grow them in a pot on my windowsill." She added, "My mom had the catalog, so I called the company. But they told me the seeds were part of a limited-time offer or something. They were totally out of them."

George glanced over at their pot of Pink Princess daisies, which was still sitting on the exhibit table. "We could split the plant in half, and you could take half with you to replant," she suggested. "I've seen my mom do that."

Viola smiled again. "Really? That would be so great!"

"If it's okay with you guys, that is," George said quickly to Nancy, Bess, and Julia.

"Viola can have some of our daisies," Bess piped up. "But not Orson! He'll do a science experiment with them and turn them into weird, ugly, yucky monster flowers!"

Nancy laughed. "Definitely!"

Sabrina
The Teenage Witch®

Salem's Tails®

What's it like to be a powerful warlock,
sentenced to one hundred years in a
cat's body for trying to take over the world?

Ask Salem.

**Read all about Salem's magical
adventures in this series based on the hit
ABC-TV show!**

A MINSTREL® BOOK
Published by Pocket Books

2007-12

The Nancy Drew Notebooks

Disappearing Daisies

"Didn't you tell me there were two categories for the children's prizes in the flower show, Nancy?" Hannah asked.

"Yes, but all we care about is the Most Beautiful Flower category, because that's the one we're going to win with our Pink Princess daisies!" Nancy said excitedly.

The phone began to ring. Hannah answered it and then handed the phone to Nancy. "It's for you."

Nancy took the phone from Hannah. "Hello?"

"Um, hello . . . Nancy?"

Nancy recognized Julia Santos's voice right away. Julia sounded upset about something.

"Oh, Nancy. It's terrible! It's the worst thing in the whole wide world!" Julia cried out. "It's the Pink Princess daisies! They're gone!"